First published in the United States, Great Britain, Canada, Australia, and New
Zealand in 2014 by NorthSouth Books Inc., an imprint of NordSüd Verlag AG,
CH-8005 Zürich, Switzerland.

Distributed in the United States by NorthSouth Books Inc., New York 10016.

Library of Congress Cataloging-in-Publication Data is available.
ISBN: 978-0-7358-4192-5
1 3 5 7 9 ◈ 10 8 6 4 2
Printed in Germany by Grafisches Centrum Cuno GmbH & Co. KG, Calbe, July 2014.

www.northsouth.com

KING
THRUSHBEARD

The Brothers Grimm *illustrated by* Irina Dobrescu

North
South

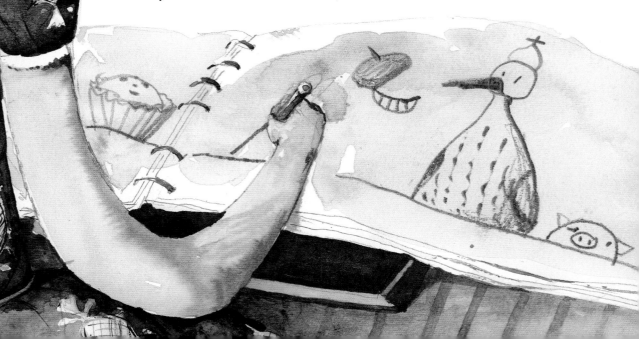

A KING had a daughter who was beautiful beyond all measure, but so proud and haughty withal that no suitor was good enough for her. She sent away one after another, and ridiculed them as well.

Once, the King made a great feast and invited thereto, from far and near, all the young men likely to marry. They were all marshaled in a row according to their rank and standing: first came the kings; then the grand dukes; then the princes, the earls, the barons, and the gentry.

Then the King's daughter was led through the ranks, but to every suitor she had some objection to make: One was too fat;

"The wine-cask," she said. Another was too tall: "Long and thin has little in." The third was too short: "Short and thick is never quick." The fourth was too pale: "As pale as death." The fifth was too red: "A fighting-cock." The sixth was not straight enough: "A green log dried behind the stove."

So she had something to say against every one, but she made herself especially merry over a good king who stood quite high up in the row, and whose chin had grown a little crooked. "Well," she cried and laughed, "he has a chin like a thrush's beak!" and from that time he got the name King Thrushbeard.

But the old King, when he saw that his daughter did nothing but mock the people, and despised all the suitors who were gathered there, was very angry, and swore that she should have for her husband the very first beggar who came to his door.

A few days afterward a fiddler came and sang beneath the windows, trying to earn a small alms. When the King heard him he said, "Let him come up." So the fiddler came in, in his dirty, ragged clothes, and sang before the King and his daughter, and when he had ended he asked for a trifling gift. The King said, "Your song has pleased me so well that I will give you my daughter, to wife."

The King's daughter shuddered, but the King said, "I have taken an oath to give you to the very first beggar-man to come to our door, and I will keep it."

All she could say was in vain; the priest was brought, and she had to let herself be wedded to the fiddler on the spot. When that was done the King said, "Now it is not proper for you, a beggar-woman, to stay any longer in my palace; you must go away with your husband."

The beggar-man led her out by the hand, and she was obliged to walk away on foot with him.

When they came to a large forest, she asked, "To whom does that beautiful forest belong?" He replied, "It belongs to King Thrushbeard; if you had taken him, it would have been yours." "Ah, unhappy girl that I am, if I had but taken King Thrushbeard!" she said.

Then they came to a large town, and she asked again, "To whom does this fine large town belong?" He replied, "It belongs to King Thrushbeard; if you had taken him, it would have been yours." "Ah, unhappy girl that I am, if I had but taken King Thrushbeard!" she said.

"It does not please me," said the fiddler, "to hear you always wishing for another husband; am I not good enough for you?"

At last they came to a very little hut, and she said, "Oh, goodness! What a small house; to whom does this miserable, tiny hovel belong?" The fiddler answered, "That is my house and yours, where we shall live together."

She had to stoop in order to go in at the low door. "Where are the servants?" said the King's daughter. "What servants?" answered the beggar-man. "You must yourself do what you wish to have done. Just make a fire at once, and set on water to cook my supper; I am quite tired." But the King's daughter knew nothing about lighting fires or cooking, and the beggar-man had to lend a hand himself to get anything fairly done. When they had finished their scanty meal they went to bed, but he forced her to get up quite early in the morning in order to look after the house.

For a few days they lived in this way as well as might be, and came to the end of all their provisions.

Then the man said, "Wife, we cannot go on any longer eating and drinking here and earning nothing. You must make baskets." He went out, cut some willows, and brought them home. Then she began to weave, but the tough willows wounded her delicate hands.

"I see that this will not do," said the man. "You had better spin; perhaps you can do that better." She sat down and tried to spin, but the hard thread soon cut her soft fingers so that the blood ran down.

"See," said the man, "you are fit for no sort of work; I have made a bad bargain with you. Now I will try to make a business with pots and earthenware; you must sit in the market-place and sell the wares." "Alas," thought she, "if any of the people from my father's kingdom come to the market and see me sitting there, selling, how they will mock me!" But it was of no use; she had to yield unless she chose to die of hunger.

For the first time she succeeded well, for the people were glad to buy the woman's wares because she was good-looking, and they paid her what she asked; many even gave her the money and left the pots with her as well. So they lived on what she had earned as long as it lasted.

Then the husband bought a lot of
new crockery. With this she sat down
at the corner of the market-place,
and set it out round about her, ready
for sale. But suddenly there came a
drunken hussar galloping along, and
he rode right among the pots so that
they were all broken into a thousand
bits. She began to weep, and did
now know what to do for fear.

"Alas! What will happen to me?" cried she. "What will my husband say to this?"

She ran home and told him of the misfortune. "Who would seat herself at a corner of the market-place with crockery?" said the man. "Leave off crying; I see very well that you cannot do any ordinary work, so I have been to our King's palace and have asked whether they cannot find a place for a kitchen-maid, and they have promised to take you; in that way you will get your food for nothing."

The King's daughter was now a kitchen-maid, and had to be at the cook's beck and call, and do the dirtiest work. In each of her pockets she fastened a little jar, in which she took home her share of the leavings, and upon this they lived.

One day it happened that the wedding of the King's eldest son was to be celebrated, so the poor woman went up and placed herself by the door of the hall to look on. When all the candles were lit, and people, each more beautiful than the one before, entered, and all was full of pomp and splendor, she thought of her lot with a sad heart, and cursed the pride and haughtiness that had humbled her and brought her to so great poverty.

The smell of the delicious dishes that were being taken in and out reached her, and now and then the servants threw her a few morsels of them; these she put in her jars to take home.

All at once the King's son entered,
clothed in velvet and silk, with gold chains about
his neck. And when he saw the beautiful woman
standing by the door he seized her by the hand, and would
have danced with her, but she refused and shrank with fear, for
she saw that it was King Thrushbeard, her suitor whom she had
driven away with scorn. Her struggles were of no avail; he drew her
into the hall, but the string by which her pockets were hung broke, the
pots fell down, the soup ran out, and the scraps were scattered all about.
And when the people saw it, there arose general laughter and derision,
and she was so ashamed that she would rather have been a thousand
fathoms below the ground.

She sprang to the door and would have run away, but on the stairs a man caught her and brought her back, and when she looked at him she saw that it was King Thrushbeard again. He said to her kindly, "Do not be afraid. I and the fiddler who has been living with you in that wretched hovel are one. For love of you I disguised myself so; and I also was the hussar who rode through your crockery. This was all done to humble your proud spirit, and to punish you for the insolence with which you mocked me."

Then she wept bitterly and said, "I have done great wrong, and am not worthy to be your wife." But he said, "Be comforted; the evil days are past. Now we will celebrate our wedding." Then the maids-in-waiting came and put on her the most splendid clothing, and her father and his whole court came and wished her happiness in her marriage with King Thrushbeard, and the joy now began in earnest. I wish you and I had been there, too.